For my brother, Rafael,
and for Lana *F.S.*

Book design by Tracey Cunnell

First published in Great Britain in 2000
by Orion Children's Books
a division of the Orion Publishing Group Ltd
Orion House
5 Upper St Martin's Lane
London WC2H 9EA

A catalogue record for this book
is available from the British Library

Miaow Miaow Bow Wow

Written by Francesca Simon
Illustrated by Emily Bolam

Orion
Children's Books

CONTENTS

Meet
The Gang

"New kid on the block! New kid on the block! Everyone meet up at Fang's!"

Do-Re-Mi the parrot squawked the news up and down Buffin Street. She flew from Prince's garden to Fang's patio, and all the way up to Millie's catflap on the third floor. She circled across the alley and even shouted the news through Moby Dick's window.

Prince the poodle stopped admiring his new blue ribbons.

Sour Puss stopped eyeing Jogger the hamster as he ran in his wheel.

Lola lifted her head from her red velvet cushion with the gold tassles and yawned.

Kit, Joey and Flick stopped yowling at each other on the alley wall.

Even Dizzy stopped chasing his tail.

"Who is it?" Dizzy asked.
Do-Re-Mi fluffed her feathers.
"A little golden puppy,"
said Do-Re-Mi.

"Great," said Dizzy. His droopy ears perked up.
"That means lots of chasing!"
"Just as long as she keeps well away
from my garden," said Prince.
"I don't want any mess."

"Where's she living?" asked Dizzy.
"At Fang's," said Do-Re-Mi. "Let's go!"

They all dashed to Fang's place to meet the newcomer.

Prince, his lovely diamond collars sparkling in the sun, ambled down to the gate between his house and Fang's.

Lily the floppy-eared rabbit burrowed out of her hutch through her secret tunnel, followed by her baby bunnies.

The alley cats Kit, Joey and Flick wriggled underneath the broken fence.

Dizzy pushed through his dog-flap and thumped down the fire escape.

Lola gazed down like a queen from her second floor balcony.

Fang met them all at the gate. He did not look very pleased.

"I suppose you've come to see *her*," he said. "Though why my people want another dog when they've got me is a mystery."
"What's she like?" asked Sour Puss, scowling. "Noisy? Dirty? Excitable?"

Honey bounced out.
"Hi, everybody!" she barked. "I'm Honey!"

"Noisy, just as I thought," grumbled Sour Puss.
She stalked off.

"Don't mind Sour Puss, she's always a bit crabby," said Do-Re-Mi. "Welcome to Buffin Street, Honey. It might look like an ordinary, every day sort of street, but it's a very special one. Come and see the sights!"

"My garden's next door," said Prince. "Keep out! And no jumping on me with muddy paws."

"Oh," said Honey. Her tail stopped wagging.

"There's lots to do at my place," said Lily, her long ears dangling almost to the ground. "We've got stepping stones to hop on and loads of flowers to nibble."

"Best digging is at the empty house next door to Prince's," said Dizzy. "I've buried lots of good bones there. And wait till you roll in the squishy mud by Foxham Pond! There are ducks to chase, and squirrels too!"

"Great!" said Honey.

"Best bins are at Bert's Beanery," said Joey. "You would not believe the delicious things he throws away! Burnt toast, sour milk, and fish heads!"

"Maybe you can join our gang," said Kit.
"When you're older," said Flick.
"Thanks!" said Honey. She thought she'd quite like to be in a gang. "What's it called?"

"The Wild Ones!"

said Kit.

"The Outlaws!"

said Joey.

"The Lizards Gizzards!"

said Flick.

"We're still deciding," said Kit.

"Best climbing trees are in front of Do-Re-Mi and Lily's home," said Millie.

"I'm not a very good climber," said Honey.

"And here's the secret hole in the broken fence," said Lily. "Perfect for sneaking out and about."

"No one knows more about escaping than Lily," said Millie. "I hope you'll come up and visit me sometime, Honey, though I do live up a lot of stairs."

"How many?" asked Honey.

She didn't like climbing lots of stairs.

Millie shrugged. "More than I can count. But if you come you can meet my friends Doris and Boris. They're the mice who live with me."

Honey's eyes opened wide. "You're friends with...mice?"

"Sure," said Millie. "What's the big deal?"

Fang looked up from where he'd been hiding his head between his paws.

"Just leave me alone," he muttered. "And don't touch my bones."

"Fang!" said Do-Re-Mi.
"That's not very kind."
"I don't care," said Fang.
"My life is ruined."

Honey bounced up to Fang.
"You won't be sorry I've come, Fang!" she barked. "Promise!"
"Huh," muttered Fang.

21

"That's all of us," said Do-Re-Mi. "We meet every Monday morning at your house, and every Friday afternoon in Foxham Park. If you need to send a message to anyone just ask me."

"How do you all get out?" asked Honey.

"We have our ways," said Do-Re-Mi softly. "There's a loose board in the fence between your house and mine that my people don't know about. Dizzy has a dog flap his person always forgets to close. And Prince can sneak out whenever he wants—he knows how to unlatch his back door."

"Wow," said Honey. This was certainly no ordinary place.

"Welcome to Buffin Street!" said Do-Re-Mi.

Yum Yum

"Lola! Here kitty, kitty, kitty! Yummy scrummy supper! Come and get it!"

Lola yawned and stretched on her red velvet cushion with the gold tassels. She hadn't moved from there all day.

Could she be bothered to slink over to her bowl and see what boring old food she was being offered?

She supposed she could.

Daintily, she sniffed at her white china bowl with her name painted in big beautiful letters.

Bleeeech! It was that revolting sea food platter in lobster jelly! No way was she eating that old slop again. And yesterday had been pheasant in gravy! Phooey! Lola was fed up with pheasant.

And tomorrow, I bet it will be so-called succulent slices of salmon, she thought, curling her lip.

I am sick and I am tired of this same old stuff, thought Lola, stalking off angrily. There has to be better food out there somewhere and I'm going to find it.

Lola climbed up the fire escape and burst through Millie's cat flap.

There was Millie, the tabby, eating her supper in the tiny kitchen.

"Hi," said Lola. "What are you eating?"

"Funky Chunky," said Millie, looking up from her chipped bowl while Doris and Boris the mice scampered about nearby. "Nothing very exciting."

"Funky Chunky?" said Lola.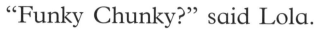
"Sounds good. Could I have a bite?"

"Sure!" said Millie. She was a little puzzled. Lola's extra special, delicious food was the talk of Buffin Street.

Lola bent down and took a tiny mouthful.

"Bleeeeechhh!" she said. "It's so dry and crackly!"

"I know," said Millie sadly.

"Listen, Millie, you have my dinner," said Lola. "I don't want it."

"What have you got?" asked Millie.

"Boring old sea food platter in lobster jelly," sighed Lola.

"Sea food platter in lobster jelly!" gasped Millie. "Oh my!"

ZIP! Millie sped off before Lola could change her mind.

Lola looked for a moment at Doris and Boris. They did look awfully plump and juicy . . . But no. Millie wouldn't like it.

Sighing, Lola padded downstairs.

Fang was snarling away as he gnawed on a bone outside his kennel on the patio.

"What *are* you eating?" said Lola.

"A yummy bone," snapped Fang, gripping it tightly in his paws. "And don't think I'm giving you a taste!"

Lola looked at the muddy, disgusting bone.

"I wouldn't want one," she said, mincing off grandly up Dizzy's stairs, her head held high.

Dizzy was guzzling his dinner.

"What are you eating?" asked Lola, peering in from the fire escape.

"Doggy Delights!" said Dizzy.
"My favourite!"

"Could I taste one?" asked Lola.

They didn't look very tempting,
but she was feeling hungry enough to try almost anything.
Moby Dick, the goldfish, was nibbling away at some very
odd-looking food, and no one had ever heard him complain.

"Go ahead," said Dizzy.

Lola delicately ate one Delight.

"Bleeeeechhh!" she said. "That tastes horrible!"

"Not to me," said Dizzy. "Yum Yum!"

Surely there was better food out there somewhere, she
thought, jumping onto the fence overlooking the alley.

Now Lola never set foot in the filthy alleyway.

Nose in the air, she strutted along the fence
towards Bert's Beanery.

Her tummy started to rumble. Where could she get something good to eat? Ah, there was Sour Puss gobbling up her dinner at Bert's back door.

"Oh Sour Puss," said Lola, slinking up. "Any chance of a taste of your—"

"EEEEYOOOOOWWWFA!" spat Sour Puss.

Lola was so terrified she slipped backwards off the fence and landed right in the alley. Eeeek, she thought, picking her way through the plastic bags, empty bottles, and greasy wrappers. What a horrid, smelly place.

There was no hope. I'll just have to starve, she thought sadly, leaping back onto the fence.

Suddenly Lola smelled something wonderful. The tempting scent made her pause. What could it be? Lola sniffed. And sniffed again.

It couldn't be—but it was. The irresistible smell was coming from Bert's bins.

Lola stiffened. She certainly wasn't going back into the alley.

Then she heard Kit, Joey and Flick squabbling inside one of the Beanery bins. Lola took one step closer.

"What are you eating?" asked Lola, peering down at them.

"Yo, Lola!" shouted Joey. "Great stuff in here! Fish heads, tuna tins, and cheese rinds! Yabadabado!"

30

Lola wrinkled her nose.

"Stop it, Joey, that's my tin!" howled Flick.

"No, mine!" yowled Joey.

"Mine!" spat Kit.

"MINE!" miaowed Lola.
And she dived head first into the bin.

"WOWEE!" said Lola, cramming her face with food. "This tastes BRILLIANT! I haven't eaten anything this good in years."

"Lola!" said Kit.
"YUMMY!" mumbled Lola,
her cheeks bulging.

"Um, Lola," hissed Joey.
CHOMP CHOMP CHOMP.

"LOLA!" screeched Flick.
"What is it?" mumbled Lola,
her cheeks bulging.

"GET AWAY FROM OUR FOOD!"
yowled the alley cats.

What an evening! A bedraggled, muddy, stinky, smelly Lola sauntered home. So what if a bath awaited?

Rampage
In Prince's
Garden

"Prince's gone!" said Fang. "I saw him drive away!"

"Where's he gone?" asked Honey. "He was bathed and clipped yesterday."

"He's gone to his other house," said Millie. "He has two, remember?"

Prince lived in Buffin Street for half the week, then somewhere else for the rest. His people shared him between them. Prince quite liked having two houses. "Twice the food, twice the presents," he always said, preening at his rows of bows, his two sparkling diamond collars and sacks full of toys.

Lola stretched and peered over her balcony.

"They've left the gate open!"

Everyone stood still as this amazing news sank in.

"Is anyone home?" asked Millie finally.

"Don't think so," said Lola.

"Are you sure?" said Sour Puss. The one time she'd tried to sneak into Prince's garden she'd been sprayed by a hose.

"Sure I'm sure," said Lola, yawning.

"I've always wanted to see Prince's secret garden," said Fang.

"Me too," said Honey.

The animals looked at each other.

"Do you think we should?" said Millie timidly.

"Sure!" said Fang. He ran to the gate and pushed it.
CR-EEEEAK! went the old gate as it swung open.
"Come on!" said Fang.
The animals looked at one another.
"We'll just take a quick peep, and then leave," said Lola.
"No harm in that," said Dizzy, his tail thumping wildly.
"Yeah," said Honey.
"No one will even know we've been there," said Millie.
In they sneaked.
"WOW!" said Fang.

"WOW!" said Lola, Dizzy, Honey, Millie and Lily.

There was a perfect, newly mown circle of lawn, with stepping stones, and little hills, and a bridge, and a goldfish pond, and statues, and piles of raked autumn leaves, and best of all, lots of freshly-dug flower beds.

Lola slinked over to the pond and eyed the fish.

Millie explored the flower-beds.

Fang found the perfect spot to hide a bone.

Lily and her bunnies started a new tunnel.

Dizzy frolicked in the leaves, chasing his tail.

"It!" shouted Honey, tapping Dizzy.

Dizzy chased after her. Then Fang joined in. And then Millie. They bounced and scampered, they zoomed and charged, racing and chasing through the leaves and flowers.

Finally, they all collapsed out of breath on the little bridge.

"That was fun!" panted Honey.

"Yeah," said Dizzy.

"Uh oh," said Millie.

"What?" said Honey.

"Look," said Millie.

"Uh oh," said Honey.

"Uh oh," said Dizzy.

Somehow the garden was wrecked.

"How did that happen?" said Millie.
"We were so careful," said Honey.
"What'll we do?" wailed Lily.

Fang took charge. "Let's tidy up quick, before Prince gets back," he ordered. "Many paws make short work."
The animals smoothed and shaped, tidied and trimmed, as fast as they could.

"There!" said Dizzy.
"Perfect!" said Fang.
A car door slammed.
"Let's get outta here!" barked Fang.
ZIP!
"No one will ever know!" said Honey.
But I am not sure that she was right.

Jogger's Big Adventure

W h e e e e ! thought Jogger the hamster, running round and round in his wheel. Now what shall I do?

He'd played in his sand bowl, tidied his bedding, raced in his wheel, and filled his hoard with food. He'd even cleaned his face. Ah! He'd gnaw on his cage door. That was always good fun.

Jogger scampered about in the wood shavings and started to chew on the bars.

NIBBLE GNAW
NIBBLE GNAW
NIBBLE GNAW

Then a strange thing happened. The door started to move. Jogger pushed. The door opened more. He pushed, and wriggled through.

THUD! Jogger landed on the ground. Oh my! This had never happened to him before when he'd gnawed on the door.

What an adventure! He'd always wondered what the world was like outside his cage. Now he'd find out.

Jogger plopped down some stairs, then found himself in a gigantic passageway. He pitter-pattered along it, then darted through a doorway. What a fascinating place!

He explored behind
the chest of drawers.

He nibbled on a book.

He swung on the duvet.

He tried climbing up a chair.

"MIAOW! MIAOW!"

Jogger peeped out from behind the chair leg. Oh no! It was that nasty Sour Puss, who always liked sitting on top of his cage and staring at him with a hungry look in her slitty eyes.

Jogger saw her sniff the air. And Jogger did not like the way she sniffed.

Hide! he thought, and darted under the bed.

Sour Puss turned and lunged at him.

BANG!

She whacked her head on the bed.

She staggered about for a moment, feeling rather dizzy.

"Jogger! Come out, come out wherever you are!" hissed Sour Puss.

No way, thought Jogger.

Suddenly two horrible green eyes blazed straight at him.

"I know you're under there," said Sour Puss. "I'll be glad to guide you back to your cage."

I don't think so, thought Jogger.

Z I P !
Jogger darted behind the bedpost.

P O U N C E !

S M A S H !
Sour Puss hit her head on the post.

"EEOWWWW!"
she squealed, her head throbbing.

I've got to get away, thought Jogger, his heart beating fast.
He darted out of the room, chased by Sour Puss.

He escaped into the toilet and hid behind the loo.

Sour Puss scurried in after him. "Aha!" said Sour Puss,
jumping on the loo.

C R A S H !

The loo seat smashed down on Sour Puss.

"OWWWW!" she yowled.

Tee hee, thought Jogger, scampering away into the kitchen.
He could outsmart that stupid cat any day.

"I'll get you!" snarled Sour Puss, staggering after him.

CLUNK!

The kitchen door swung shut in her face.

"EOOWWWWWW!"

Jogger looked round and sighed.

Wow, that was close, he thought, his heart pounding. Safe at last. Sour Puss couldn't get him now. He'd have a sniff round, then find his way back home.

Suddenly the cat flap started to move.

"Gotcha!"

miaowed Sour Puss, wriggling through the flap.

Jogger froze.

"EEEEEEEE!" he squeaked.

Sour Puss was in the room.

"Help!"

Sour Puss got ready to leap. He was dead. Goodbye world!

Suddenly a giant hand scooped him up.
"Jogger, what are you doing here?"
Phew, thought Jogger. What a lucky escape.
Once safely back in his cage, Jogger went straight to his little house and buried himself in the bedding. He'd had enough adventures—for that day, anyway.

Look At Me

A few weeks later, Do-Re-Mi brought great news to Buffin Street.

"Foxham Pond's frozen over! Foxham Pond's frozen over!" she squawked.

"Says who?" asked Prince.

"The ducks!" said Do-Re-Mi. "And they should know."

"Yippee!" said Fang.
"Yippee!" echoed Honey.
Then she stopped.
"What's so great about that?"

"Come on Honey!" said Millie. "We're going skating!"

"Skating?" said Honey. She'd never been skating before and wasn't sure she wanted to.

"Don't worry, you'll love it," said Millie.

Late that night, the animals slipped out into the cold, frosty darkness. Buffin Street was silver and silent, dusted in snow.

Carefully, they crossed the road, trotted past the dry cleaners, the corner shop, the church and the playground and scampered into the park. There was Foxham Pond, a gleaming sheet of ice.

"Let's go, Honey!" shouted Millie. She bounded onto the ice whizzing and whirling with the others.

53

Honey stared at the twirling skaters. Then, carefully, she put her front paws onto the ice. Brrr! It was cold.

She slid out one paw and skidded.

Wh$_{oo}$ps!

Honey tried again.

Wh$_{oo}$ps!

And again.
Suddenly Honey started sliding across the ice.

"Look out!
I can't stop!"
she shouted.

Crash!

"Watch where you're going!" spat Sour Puss.
"Sorry," said Honey. This wasn't fun at all. Fang hurtled by.
"I'm the best! I'm the best skater in the world," shouted Fang.
Round and round he whizzed.

"Wheee!
Look at me!"
shouted Fang.
"I'm amazing!"

Honey turned away and limped off the ice, slipping and sliding.

"I don't want to skate anymore," said Honey. Fang could zoom about and she couldn't even get four paws on the ice without falling.

Someone flashed by. It was Prince.

Fang stopped skating and stared.

Prince swooped and looped and whirled and twirled.

"Wow, look at Prince," said Honey.

Fang turned away.

"Huh," he said. "What a show-off. I'm tired of skating anyway. I'm going home."

"Wheee!
Look at me!"
shouted Prince, prancing and dancing.
"I'm amazing!"

Someone else flashed by. It was Milly.
Prince stopped skating and stared.
Flick be-bopped and hopped, shimmied and streaked.
Honey could not believe her eyes.
"Wow, look at Flick," she said.
Prince turned up his nose and walked off the ice.

"Wheee!
Look at me!"
shouted Flick,
"I'm amazing!"

Honey sat for a moment. Then she got up and walked onto the ice.

W o b b l e...

wh o o p s! Down she crashed.

She got to her feet and tried again.

Wo^b^b^le...

wo^b^ble...

wh~oo~ps!

And then...

Wo^bb^le...

Wo^bb^le...

Wheeeeeeeee!

Honey was on all fours. She was gliding. She was sliding.
And she wasn't falling. She was skating!

"Wheee! Look at me!" shouted Honey.
"I'm amazing!"

The Haunted House Of Buffin Street

"You're joking," said Honey.

"Would I joke about something so awful?" said Fang.

"But it can't be true!" said Honey. "I like it here. I don't want to move."

"What we want doesn't matter," said Fang sadly.

"*They* want to move and there's nothing we can do about it."

"But why move?" said Honey.

"They want a house with a garden," said Fang.

"A garden?" said Honey, perking up for a moment. Then she sighed again.

"I'd rather stay in Buffin Street with our little patio than have a garden," she said.

Prince poked his nose through the fence.
"Bad news, eh?" he said.
"The worst," said Fang.
"What about me?" said Prince. "I don't want new neighbours. For all I know the new ones might hate dogs. Or worse, have a horrible yappy dog themselves. Or" —he groaned—"a cat."

"Nothing wrong with cats," said Millie, leaping down the fire escape.
"Cats are purrrrfect," said Lola.
"Ha," said Prince, bristling.

"Stop it you two," said Do-Re-Mi, flying down from the window. "The main thing is, how can we keep Fang and Honey here?"

Everyone stood in silence.

"It's hopeless," said Fang. "The new people are coming tonight to look round one last time and sign the papers. It's too late."

"No it isn't," said Millie suddenly. "I've got a plan that just might work."

Everyone stared at Millie. It wasn't like her to have a plan.

"Well, let's hear it," said Fang.

Do-Re-Mi saw the new people walking down Buffin Street and squawked a warning.

"They're coming!" said Lola.
"Positions, everyone!" said Millie.

Prince started howling.

"AWHOOOOO!
AWHOOOOO!"

Then Dizzy did too.

"AWHOOOOO!
AWHOOOOO!"

Then the Alley Cats joined in.

"MIAOW YOW YOW!
MIAOW YOW YOW!"

"What a noisy street," said the woman.
"I had no idea," said the man, ringing Fang's door bell.

The animals heard the door open, and then footsteps coming down the hall.

"Doris and Boris first!" whispered Millie.

The mice skittered across the room.

"EEEEEK! Mice!" squealed the woman.

"Disgusting!" shouted the man.

"Go for it!" said Millie.

"OOOOOOOOooooOOOOOO!" moaned Fang.

"OOOOOOOOooooOOOOOO!" moaned Honey.

"SSSSSSSss!" hissed Lola and Millie, their swishing tails making the curtains sway.

"SCR$_A$A^{A}A$_A$A$_A$ATCH!" went Lily's sharp claws on the wooden floor.

The people froze.

"What's that noise?" said the woman.

"I don't know," said the man.

"OOOOOOOOOOOOOOOOOO!" moaned Fang and Honey.

"I don't like this," said the woman.

"SSSSSSSsssssssSSSSSSSS," hissed Lola and Millie, a little louder.

"SCR_AA_AA_ATCH!" scraped Lily's claws.

Suddenly Do-Re-Mi swooped.

"SQUAWK! SQUAWK! SQUAWK! GO AWAY!" she screeched.

"AAAAHHHH!" shrieked the people. "The house is haunted! HELP!"

And they ran screaming out of the door.
"We did it!" cheered the animals. "Three cheers for Millie!"
"It was nothing, really," said Millie, hanging her head shyly.

After this Fang and Honey's haunted house became famous up and down Buffin Street. No one wanted to move there. Which suited the animals just fine.

Miaow Miaow Bow Wow

"MIAOW Yow Yow!
MIAOW Yow Yow!
MIAOWWWWW—Yow!"

Every night Kit, Joey and Flick entertained Buffin Street with their Alley Cat Chorus.

Sometimes Millie sang along from her third floor window.
"ME ME ME ME YOWWWW!"

Sometimes Sour Puss did, too.
"MEE E$_E$E E$_E$E E$_E$E YOWWW!"

Sometimes even the people who lived in Buffin Street joined in.

Be Quiet!

Shooo!

Dizzy thought the Alley Cats sounded wonderful.

I wish I could sing with them, he said to himself. Why should cats have all the fun?

Next day he went over to the alley. The cats were skulking around the bins, as usual.

"Please could I join the chorus?" said Dizzy.

The cats looked at one another.

"But you're a dog," said Flick. "This is an alley CAT chorus."

"So?" said Dizzy. "Just wait till you hear me sing."

Dizzy opened his mouth.

"AWHOOOOOO! AWHOOOOO!
BOW WOW WOW WOW WOW!"

he barked, tail thumping with happiness.

The cats covered their ears.

"BOW WOWW—"

"Stop that terrible noise!" said Joey.

"Oh my aching ears!" moaned Kit.

"Sorry, Dizzy, you're just not good enough to sing with the Alley Cats," said Flick, leaping into an old crate.

Dizzy's tail stopped thumping. He felt so upset he slunk home as fast as he could.

He hid behind the sofa where he thought no one would see him, and felt very sorry for himself. He looked so sad that Moby Dick, swimming round and round his goldfish bowl, wished he could help.

But then Dizzy started to think.

And then he started to get angry.

What do those stupid cats know, anyway, about singing? They wouldn't know a fine voice if it bopped them on the head.

And then Dizzy had a wonderful idea. He leapt out from behind the sofa, barked goodbye to Moby Dick, and ran downstairs to see his next-door neighbours, Fang and Honey.

"Let's start a dog chorus!" he said. "I'm sure we'd sing much better than those screechy Alley Cats."
"Sure," said Fang.
"Why not?" said Honey, who always did whatever Fang did.
"I'll give it a try," said Prince from his garden gate. "If I'm free."

"I thought we'd call ourselves the Doggie Delights," said Dizzy. What could be nicer than a chorus named after his favourite food?
Everyone agreed that was a wonderful name.

The Doggie Delights decided to have their first sing-a-long that night, when all their people were in bed.

At midnight everyone sneaked out and gathered on Fang's patio.

"AWHOOOOOO!
AWHOOOOO!
BOW WOW
WOW WOW
WOW!"

howled the Doggie Delights.

Silence.

Then from the alley came a familiar chorus.

"MIAOW
YOW YOW!
MIAOW
YOW YOW!
MIAOWWWWWW—YOW!"

"Louder, Delights!" barked Dizzy.

"AWHOOOOOOOO!
AWHOOOOO!
BOW WOW
WOW WOW
WOWWWWW!"

bellowed the dogs.

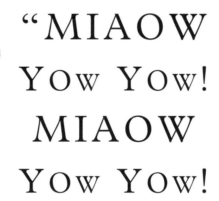

"MIAOW
YOW YOW!
MIAOW
YOW YOW!
MIAOWWWWWW—YOW!"

screeched the cats.

Louder and louder they sang, each trying to drown out
the other.

"MIAOW MIAOW BOW WOW" echoed up and down Buffin Street."

They miaowed and bow wowed until dawn, then settled down for a well-earned sleep.

In the afternoon Dizzy went for a walk to Foxham Park. He felt sleepy, but happy. What a great night's singing they'd had! He was glad the Buffin Street people had really enjoyed themselves too, considering how often they'd joined in. The Doggie Delights sounded brilliant, much better than the Alley Cats. He couldn't wait to do it again.

Flick blocked his way on the corner.

"We've got to talk," said Flick.

"Yeah," said Joey and Kit, appearing on the wall.

"What about?" asked Dizzy.

"You spoiled our chorus last night," said Flick.

"Well you spoiled ours," said Dizzy.

"We sang first," hissed the cats.

"So?" said Dizzy. The fur on his neck started rising.

Do-Re-Mi flew over.

"Friends! Friends! This is no way to behave.
We've always got along well on Buffin Street!"

"The street's not big enough for two chorus'," spat Kit.

Do-Re-Mi thought for a moment.

"I've got an idea," she said. "What if the Alley Cats sing
Mondays, Wednesdays, and Fridays, and the Doggie Delights
Tuesdays, Thursdays, and Saturdays?"

"What about Sundays?" said Dizzy.

"Joint concert!" said Do-Re-Mi.

And that's exactly what you'll hear, should you stroll along Buffin Street late at night on a Sunday.

"MIAOW MIAOW BOW WOW!"

"MIAOW MIAOW BOW WOW!"